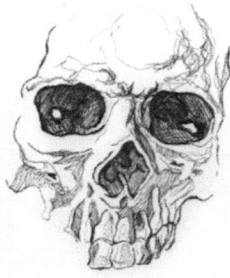

Dear Lucy,

As it will be some time before everything gets back to normal and I realize that it will now be in the new year at the earliest before normality returns I have taken the liberty to send you this book.
The first Christmas with a new family is always special as children light up the day in a way that only children can.
I realise, as I am sure you will also, that this book is not for now but for future years, at bedtime stories.
I myself have three daughters and they have been a great source of love, amusement and support through the years.
Christmas is always the best of times.

I wish you and your family a happy and wonderful Christmas and new year.

Hope you don't mind
Looking forward to returning to PH in the near future.

Best wishes

Doug

Contents

Foreword.

For those who believe in their own imaginations...

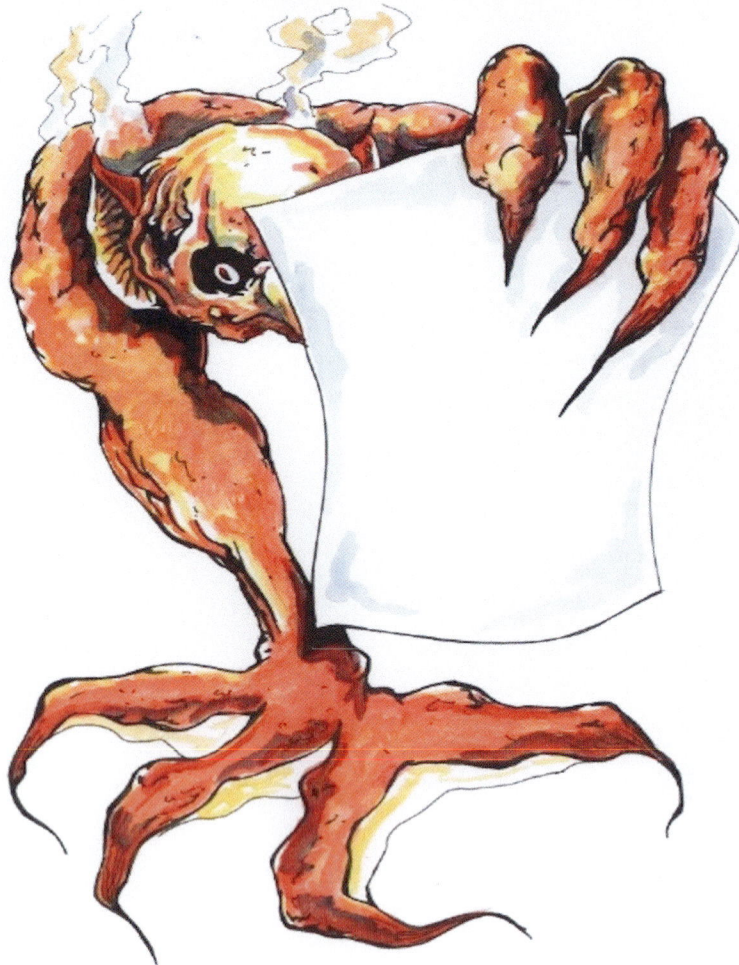

Dedication

For

Jassy, Alex & Cara

No matter how old we become a small part of us always remains a child.

DEMONS & THINGS

Demons and Things.

Lizards and newts, frogs and toads, demons and gorgons all in a line dressed for dinner all looking so fine.

Dinners at twelve, the witches' hour held in a room at the top of a tower. All manner of creatures will be there, come to see old friends, to look and to stare. Magic abounds it crackles around, rabbits from top hats, pigeons from sleeves, some sleight of hand that always deceives.

The Grand Master is there at the top of the table looking quite splendid, majestic and able. He'll conjure up spirits and rats from the air, he'll turn you to jelly without a care. If you're not careful to lend your ear, well, he'll turn rather nasty and you'll disappear. Now music begins after dinner is done and there's dancing and things, it's all such fun.

But when dawn starts to break and the sun begins to rise, it's time for these creatures to shield their eyes. And it's back to the darkness where they came from to wait until midnight to start again...

Dreamy Meals.

Of all the creatures in this world the kind I like
the most is the kind you eat with honey or spread
with jam on toast.
To feel this tasty treat go down, my mouth
begins to droll. I like this food in cold meat pies
or piping hot in gruel. As a bedtime snack I think
it's grand with hot milk by the fire. It's the kind
of food that's rare you know but it's the kind that
I desire. It's hard to come by although there's
lots of it about. I used to get it by the woods or
by the castle moat. O, I think I'll take a walk
outside, maybe take a stroll but it's getting harder
to catch this dish for an ancient weary Troll.

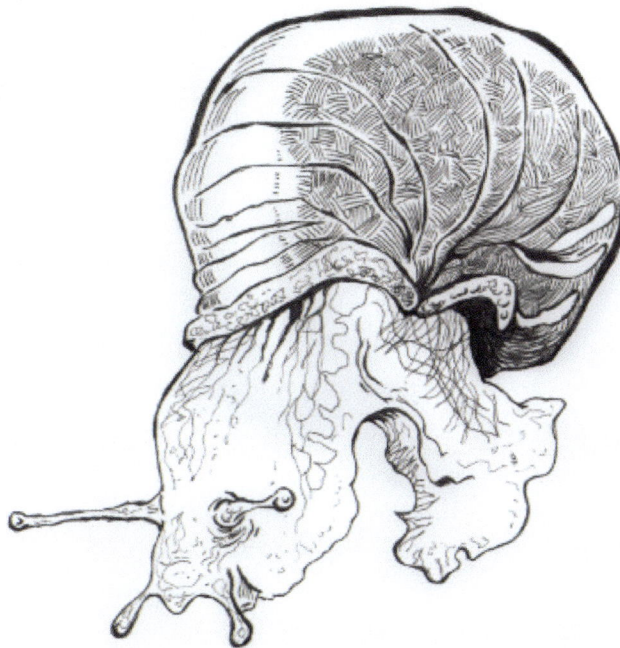

ONE
OF
MINE

One of Mine.

It was yesterday in the school yard you seemed to pass me by.
You seemed to look right through me, me thinking you were shy.
Your socks were loose, down by your shoes, your laces all undone.
A cut upon your knee, your tie was missing, and your coat was all askew.
You really looked a terrible fool.
A smile it came across your face and your hair was hanging in the wrong place.
I looked at you just standing there, the ribbons escaping from your hair.
Then your eyes they seemed to sparkle and then began to shine and that is why I love you,
This wonderful daughter of mine.

Winters' Tale.

There's a cold wind blowing around our house, everyone's inside even that darn mouse. Jack Frost at the window, the North Wind at the door and dad is by the fire while the cat is on the floor.

Mum's making soup to keep us nice and warm, so let's forget about the weather and the raging storm. Now snow begins to fall in fine white flakes, it's landing on the garden and outside our gate. The fire is blazing nicely and I'm cosy and snug and dad will read us stories, sipping hot chocolate from his mug. When it's time to go to bed I'll laugh and mess about then dad and mum will holler – *everyone will shout!*

Then I will be a good child and kiss and say goodnight. Mum will take me up to bed tucking me in tight. I'll listen to the wind as I lay upon my bed and think of all the good things inside my head. I might even dream of Christmas when Santa comes to call, sliding down the chimney careful not to fall. So, I think I'll close my eyes now and try to go to sleep
And God bless everyone and make not a peep.

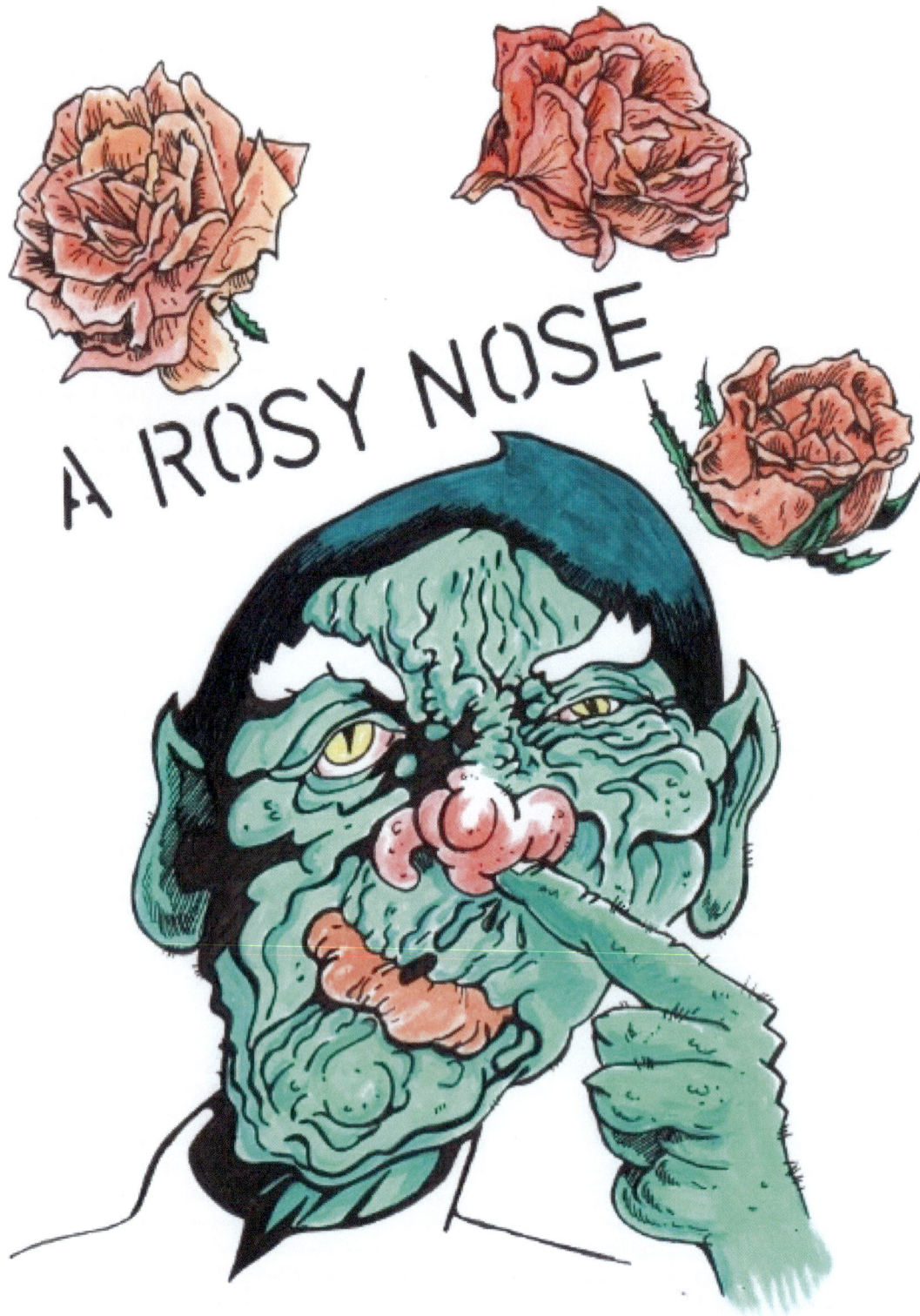

A ROSY NOSE

A Rosy Nose.

A Rose, a Rose...Aww! stop picking your nose
And try to be what dreams are made of.
Be moody
Be sad
Then happy and mad
A joy to be with.
Try to be my heart's desire
Try to set this soul on fire.
Oh! Jeez! Stop picking your nose
And wiping it under the table.
This habit of yours almost blew it!
I'm grateful you didn't chew it!
Be romantic, steamy and frantic...
On second thoughts...

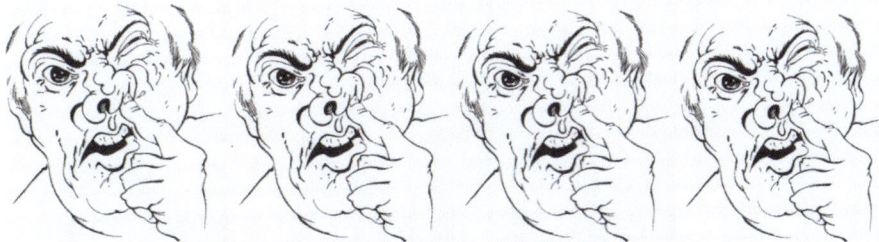

...GO PICK YOUR NOSE!

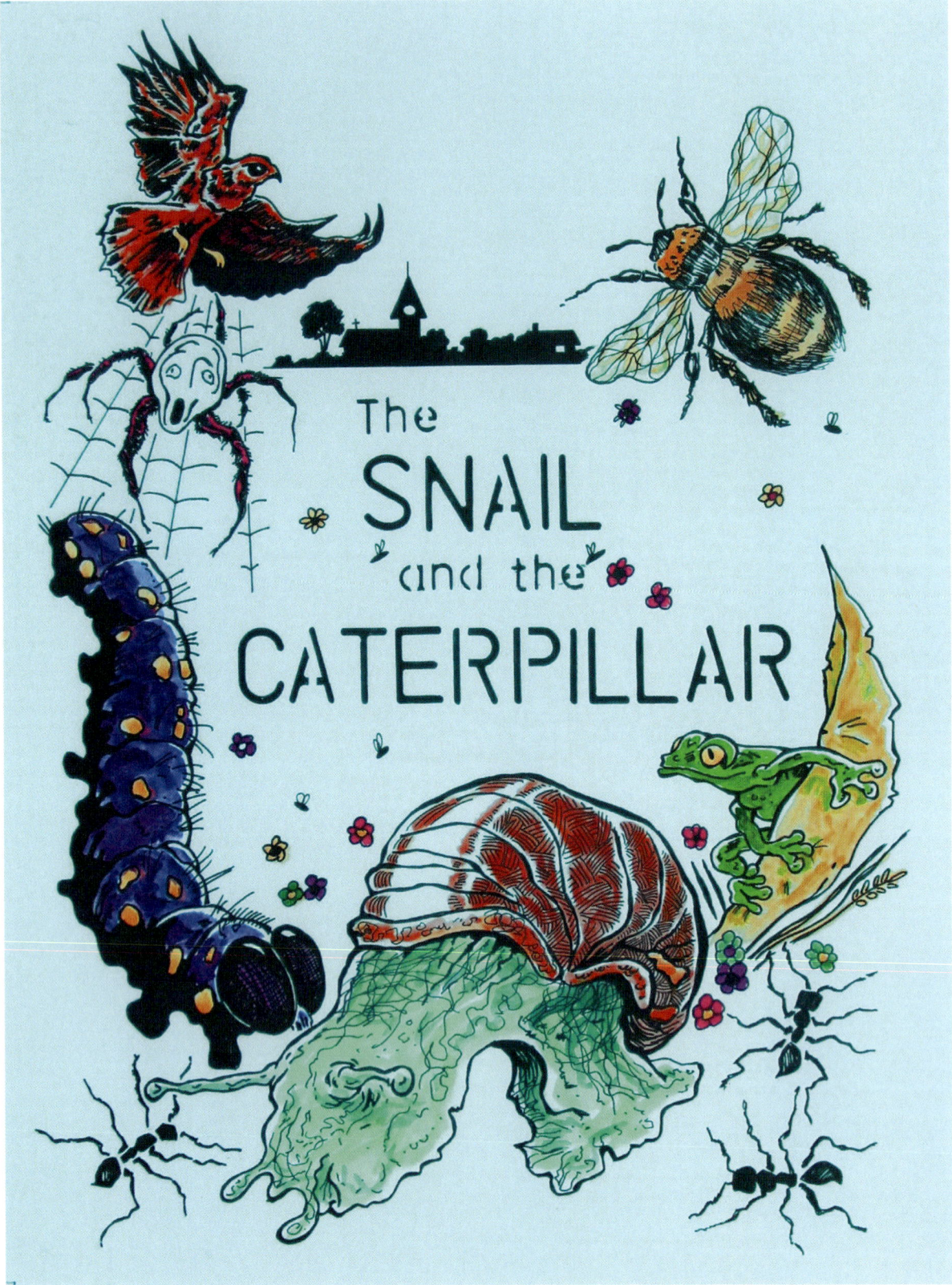

The
SNAIL
and the
CATERPILLAR

The Snail and the Caterpillar.

The Snail and the Caterpillar were soon to be wed, all creatures great and small would be there it was said.

The Damson Fly and Dragon Fly put on their best wings whilst the Hornet and Wasp just polished their stings.

The church bells were ringing in a small country town while the Caterpillar was grooming and cleaning her gown.

The Snail washed his body and stalk like eyes "A snail fit to marry," a large bird sighs.

The bee was too busy to even attend, collecting all the honey drove him clean around the bend.

He was flitting from flower to flower, working away passing hour by hour.

When he went home at the dusk of the day The Snail and the Caterpillar were wed and away.

A honeymoon is grand thing as Ants will tell...

...but fancy being married to a Caterpillar or Snail.

Thomas O'Flynn

…always had a big grin.

Thomas O'Flynn always had a big grin
As down to the sea he would go.
Arrive in the morning
Without any warning
Loaded with contraptions galore
The breeze in his face as he stepped out apace
His eager heart pounding with joy.

He loved this new sport; the one he was taught whilst on holiday you know, it was last summer you see and changing as fast as could be, for a while naked he stood as he slipped into his gear, his grin begun to spread... from ear to ear.

He thought he looked grand as he took to his hand a surfboard, glistening and new. With a smile on his face into the sea he did race leaving all of his cares far behind. Left on the shore his clothes moving no more to show where Thomas had been.

A monument... to Thomas O'Flynn.

Now Thomas O'Flynn who had a big grin was also known for the size of his head and it was this, it was said, because of its size that lead to poor Tommy demise. The size and the weight may have led to his fate but really, it's only a guess. For Thomas was seen to look cool and mean, for on top he wore only a vest.

Now his Life Jacket he'd completely forgot.
They found the said garment back in his
apartment which explains why Thomas never
came back. Let us return to the sea with Thomas
so full of glee hurtling over the waves. The wind
in his hair, spray leaving a trail, gliding over a
crest in his stringy white vest Thomas sailed to
the edge of the world.

If your down by the beach as the clouds roll on by and the wind starts to whistle a tune, look up over your head for tis true, it is said, you may see Thomas sailing on by...

...his grin as broad as the sky.

SPACEMAN, POLICEMAN.

A Policeman was out walking upon his beat one day when he chanced to meet a Spaceman who was passing by that way. The Spaceman greeted the P.C as polite as he could be, the Policeman returned the same and asked him home for tea.

As they sat and ate cream cakes and pouring cups of tea, the Policeman asked the Spaceman "What's the trouble, lad? Come now, you can tell me!" *"It appears to be my spacecraft, broken down you see!"* came Spaceman's quick reply.
Then Spaceman grinned and laughed aloud and wiped his every eye. "What the joke?" asked Policeman, "It doesn't sound funny to me!"

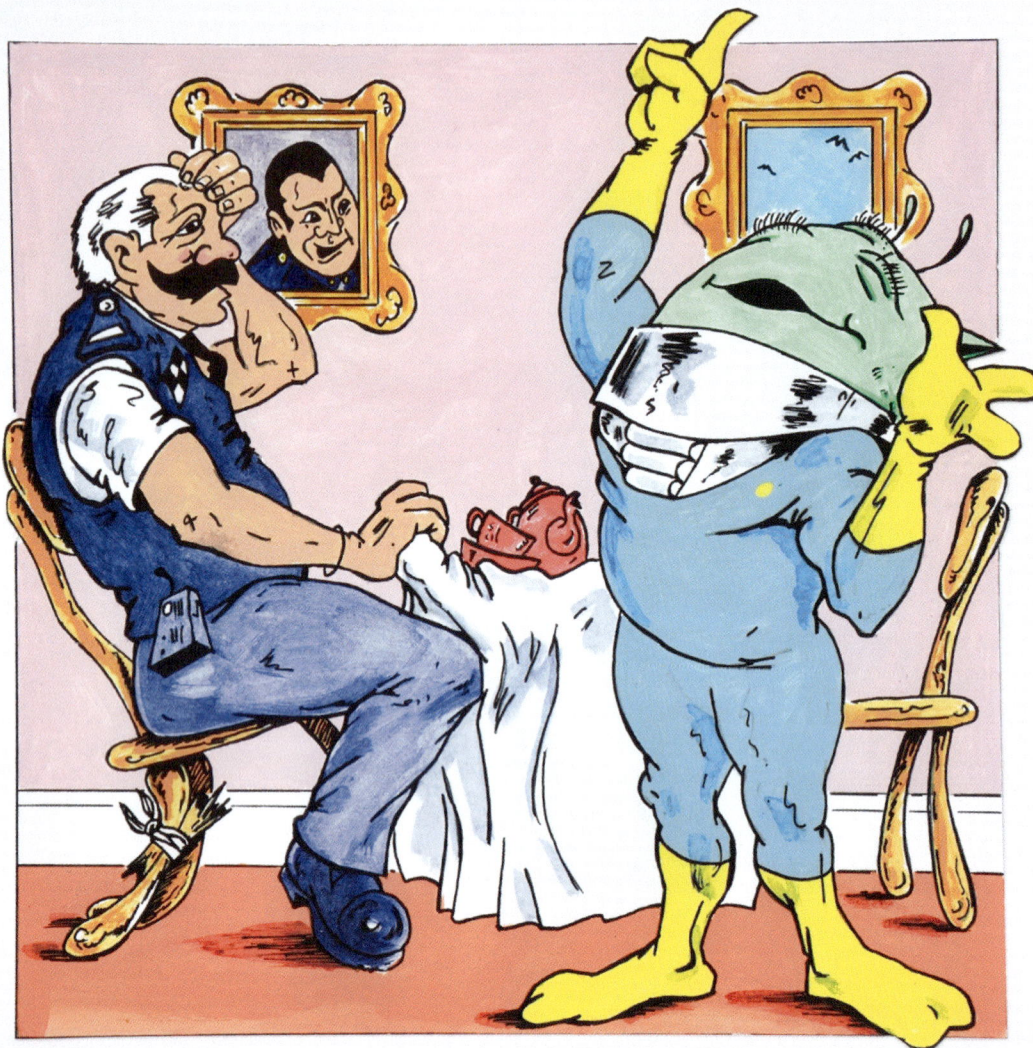

"Your just not what I expected an alien to be."

Now Policeman grinned and saw the joke of which you'll all agree, "I see your point," said Policeman "Is the alien you or me!" After tea they both got up and strolled back to the spot where Spaceman's craft had landed, for it is a Policeman's lot to help someone in trouble, assist in all he can and make your day a better

one by lending a helping hand. The Policeman took his coat off and rolling up his sleeves said, "Stand aside and let me see what yonder trouble can be!" He pulled a wire here and there and turned some nuts and bolts pulling out all manner of things, you could hear him spit and curse. The Spaceman looking on, could see that things were getting worse.

"I think it's very kind of you to try to help this way but there is just one thing that I would like to say. It's not the engine broken down which is spread around your feet. It merely needed water to take away the heat."

"Only over Heating!" our P.C meekly said and looking at the mess he'd made he stood and scratched his head.

"*Never mind,*" said Spaceman *"I have a friend in here whose very good at fixing things, whose trust I hold quite dear."* From a small compartment a creature did appear who picked up all the engines parts and threw them into gear. It didn't take him long you see as the creature whirled on past for robots work as robots work and robots work quite fast.

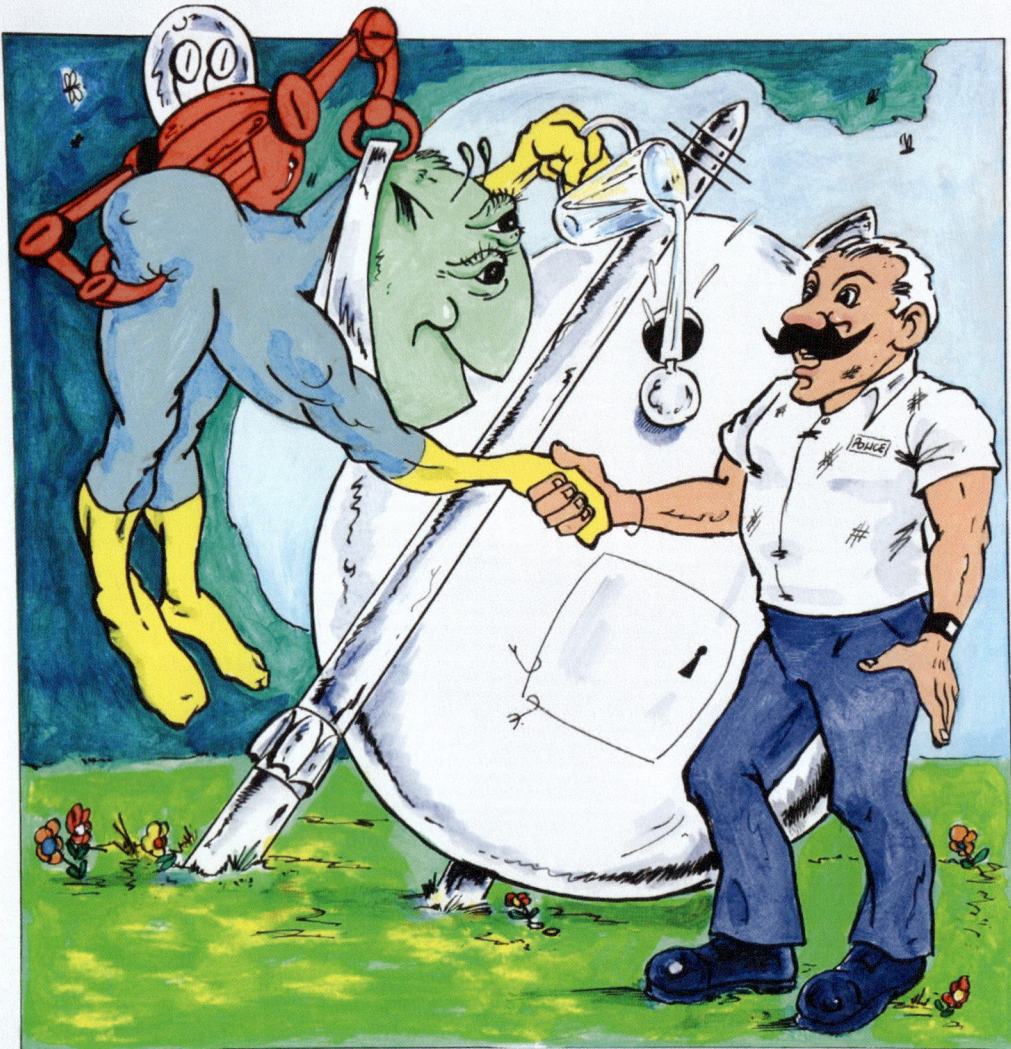

The Policeman feeling quite embarrassed stood
and gave a cry, "I know where we can get some
water as there's a stream that runs close by!"
So Spaceman and Policeman set off with a pail
and wandered through the woods and down a
rustic trail. Returning with the water and finding
robot done, they topped up Spaceman's craft and
shook hands everyone.

Spaceman and his robot climbed back into his craft and starting up the engine he smiled and gave a laugh. The Policeman waved and smiled goodbye, for spaceman the stars began to call, and all that Policeman could think to say was...

...''Evenin ' all!''

A poem for today.

I met a man upon my way
A happy man I have to say
I noticed, as you do
He had three legs...not two!
A funny thought went through my head
So this is what I went and said
"What do you do when you want socks?
For socks they come in only two's"
And this became he's quick reply
"I swap them two with one and back to three,
for this small task amuses me."
I thought this was a cunning plan
Coming from such a man,
He, with his three legs not two
For I suppose that's what you do.
I asked if he would walk with me
As I was going to the fair
A chance to meet some people there.
We walked along unto the fair
and met a throng of people there.
Some they stared with all their might
Some they screamed and then took flight.
He seemed unfazed, two legs or three,
It was all the same to He.

He didn't walk to the left
He didn't walk to the right
Sometimes backwards...what a sight!
When he walked motioned to the fore
He seemed to wander, O I don't know,
He didn't care which way to go.
But he looked the same as you and me
Except of course his legs of three.
When he left he waved goodbye
and shook my hand
and what he said you'll understand,
" When I leave, I think you'll find that previous
notions you'll leave behind. "

I think about him now and then and wonder if
we'll meet again.
So if you see this man who walks upon this sorry
land with his three legs, not two
Should it matter much to you?
He looks the same as you and me
Except of course his legs of three.

About the author.

I was born in the city of Portsmouth, Hampshire, England, UK in 1950.

From an early childhood I have always liked stories and fantasies, or fables if you will. I did not indulge in poetry until my late teens although I had a secret joy of English, as a written word, whilst in my secondary schooling. I was not a great reader of books and indeed did not really lift a book off a shelve until getting married in 1974.

I did however enjoy several Shakespeare plays broadcast on BBC during the 60's and still hold an affection for these but I do not find Shakespeare an easy read.

My wife, being an avid reader herself passed on to me some of her old novels and so started me on the reading trail.

The use of the English language by such giants as H G Wells or Charles Dickens are a favourite and over the years I have been immersed in such classics as War of the Worlds, The Invisible Man, The First Men in the Moon, Westward Ho (Charles Kingsley), Ivanhoe (Walter Scott) and not forgetting The Three Musketeers (Alexandre Dumas) as well as the many classics by Dickens. More modern authors such as Frank Yerby (Judas My Brother, Swan Song) and long forgotten, Michael Moorcock (Chronicles of Count Brass & The Magic Amulet), Stuart Turton (The Seven Deaths of Evelyn Hardcastle), Susanna Clarke (The Ladies of Grace Adieu), George Macdonald Fraser (the Flashman series) have all been great reads.

When one reads a book and enjoys it so much it imbeds itself into your subconscious and in doing so enhances your anticipation to your next book.

I also enjoy a passion for drawing and most things *"Arty"* and indulge in Life Drawing, painting and sculpture having won two awards with **The American Arts Awards International Open** (online) in 2017-2018 placed 6th (2017) and 5th (2018).
I am a former member of **The National Society of Painters, Sculptors & Printmakers** based in London having shown works at various exhibitions over the years. I have had work displayed with **The Royal Society of British Artists 'Open'** exhibition in **The Mall Galleries, London** (2012), which was for me, a great highlight for that year.

It wasn't until my three daughters were born that I took up a pen and wrote poems to amuse them (and to be truthful, myself as well) at bedtime. The short tales or poems within this book are unchanged of word (ok, I may have dabbled a bit with the odd line) and hopefully still hold a little charm even after several decades. The illustrations are new except for Thomas O'Flynn and Spaceman, Policeman of which I have stuck to my original drawings from the 70's as near as I could adding only colour.

You will find another small book of poems by myself on Amazon Kindle and a paperback version called 'Another Side of Me'.
This particular book is for persons over a certain age which looks at love, war and inevitably death.

I wish you good reading.

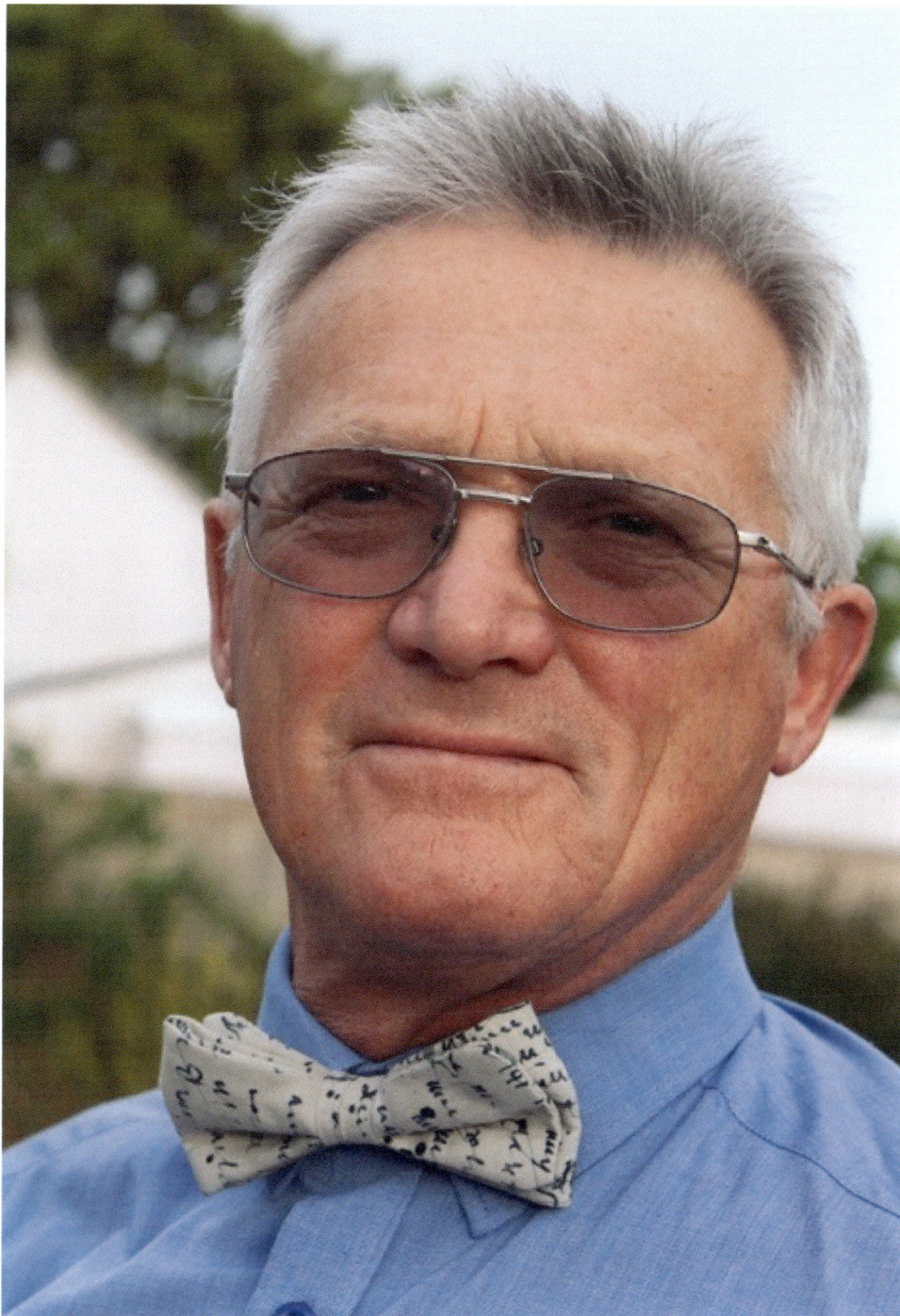

Lawrence Douglas S Davis

**All text and illustrations/artwork
By
Lawrence Douglas Davis.**

ISBN:9781792633553.

Another side of me

A selection of poems

by

Lawrence Douglas Davis

A selection of drawings, some used and some not, for this publication.

Demons and Things

A book of
childrens poems

by

Lawrence Douglas
Davis

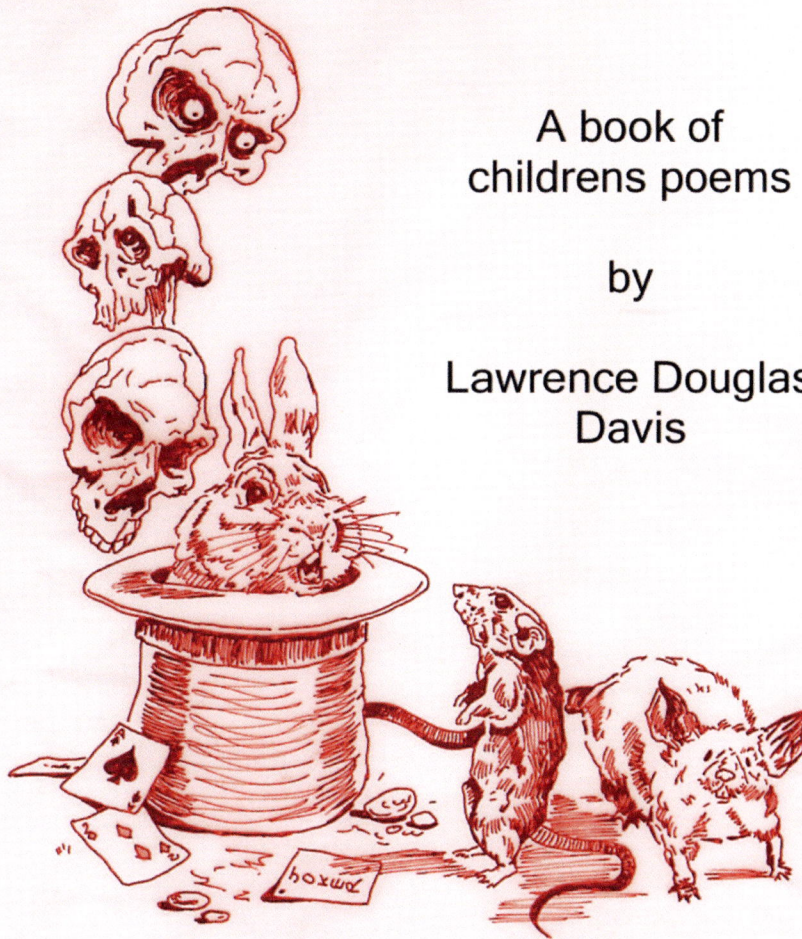

Original cover design in pink.

Printed in Poland
by Amazon Fulfillment
Poland Sp. z o.o., Wrocław